THE SILVER BOX

THE SILVER BOX

John Galsworthy

MAPLE PRESS

The Silver Box

Script Edition - 2011

Author : John Galsworthy

Published by : Koncept Books, Dehradun (Uttarakhand)

Marketed by : Maple Press, H-205, Sector-63, NOIDA - 201307 (U.P.)
☎ (0120) - 4267184 Telefax : 4267183
Website : www.maplepress.co.in
e-mail : info@maplepress.co.in

Printed By : DD Offset Printing Press, Noida

CONTENTS

ABOUT THE AUTHOR

John Galsworthy (1867-1933)

John Galsworthy was educated at Harrow and studied law at New College, Oxford. He travelled widely and at the age of twenty-eight began to write, at first for his own amusement. His first stories were published under the pseudonym John Sinjohn and later were withdrawn. He considered *The Island Pharisees* (1904) his first important work. As a novelist Galsworthy is chiefly known for his *roman fleuve, The Forsyte Saga.* The first novel of this vast work appeared in 1906. *The Man of Property* was a harsh criticism of the upper middle classes, Galsworthy's own background, Galsworthy did not immediately continue it; fifteen years and with them the First World War intervened until he resumed work on the history of the Forsytes with *In Chancery* (1920) and *To Let* (1921). Meanwhile he had written a considerable number of novels, short stories, and plays. *The Forsyte Saga* was continued by the three volumes of *A Modern Comedy, The White Monkey* (1924), *The Silver Spoon* (1926), *Swan Song* (1928), and its two interludes *A Silent Wooing* and *Passsersby* (1927). To these should be added *On Forsyte Change* (1930), a collection of short stories. With growing age

Galsworthy came more and more to identify himself with the world of his novels, which at first he had judged very harshly. This development is nowhere more evident than in the author's changing attitude toward Soames Forsyte, the "man of property," who dominates the first part of the work.

Galsworthy was a dramatist of considerable technical skill. His plays often took up specific social grievances such as the double standard of justice as applied to the upper and lower classes in *The Silver box* (1906) and the confrontation of capital and labour in *Strife* (1909). *Justice* (1910), his most famous play, led to a prison reform in England. Galsworthy's reaction to the First World War found its expression in *The Mob* (1914), in which the voice of a statesman is drowned in the madness of the war-hungry masses; and in enmity of the two families of *The Skin Game* (1920).

John Galsworthy died on January 31, 1933.

PERSONS OF THE PLAY

JOHN BARTHWICK, M.P., *a wealthy Liberal*
MRS. BARTHWICK, *his wife*
JACK BARTHWICK, *their son*
ROPER, *their solicitor*
MRS. JONES, *their charwoman*
MARLOW, *their manservant*
WHEELER, *their maidservant*
JONES, *the stranger within their gates*
MRS. SEDDON, *a landlady*
SNOW, *a detective*
A POLICE MAGISTRATE
AN UNKNOWN LADY, *from beyond*
TWO LITTLE GIRLS, *homeless*
LIVENS, *their father*
A RELIEVING OFFICER
A MAGISTRATE'S CLERK
AN USHER
POLICEMEN, CLERKS, AND OTHERS

TIME: The present. The action of the first two Acts takes place on Easter Tuesday; the action of the third on Easter Wednesday week.

ACT I., SCENE I. *Rockingham Gate. John Barthwick's dining-room.*
SCENE II. *The same.*
SCENE III. *The same.*

ACT II., SCENE I. *The Jones's lodgings, Merthyr Street.*
SCENE II. *John Barthwick's dining-room.*

ACT III. *A London police court.*

ACT I

SCENE I

The curtain rises on the BARTHWICK'S *dining-room, large, modern, and well furnished; the window curtains drawn. Electric light is burning. On the large round dining-table is set out a tray with whisky, a syphon, and a silver cigarette-box. It is past midnight. A fumbling is heard outside the door. It is opened suddenly;* JACK BARTHWICK *seems to fall into the room. He stands holding by the door knob, staring before him, with a beatific smile. He is in evening dress and opera hat, and carries in his hand a sky-blue velvet lady's reticule. His boyish face is freshly coloured and clean-shaven. An overcoat is hanging on his arm.*

JACK : Hello! I've got home all ri——[*Defiantly.*] Who says I sh'd never 've opened th' door without 'sistance. [*He staggers in, fumbling with the reticule. A lady's handkerchief and purse of crimson silk fall out.*] Serve her joll' well right—everything droppin' out. Th' cat. I've scored her off—I've got her bag. [*He swings the reticule.*] Serves her joly' well right. [*He takes a cigarette out of the silver box and puts it in his mouth.*] Never gave tha' fellow anything! [*He hunts through all his pockets and pulls a shilling out; it drops and rolls away. He looks for it.*] Beastly shilling! [*He looks again.*] Base ingratitude! Absolutely nothing. [*He laughs.*] Mus' tell him I've got absolutely nothing.

[*He lurches through the door and down a corridor, and presently returns, followed by* JONES, *who is advanced in liquor.* JONES, *about thirty years of age, has hollow cheeks, black circles round his eyes, and rusty clothes: He looks as though he might be unemployed, and enters in a hang-dog manner.*]

JACK : Sh! sh! sh! Don't you make a noise, whatever you do. Shu' the door, an' have a drink. [*Very solemnly.*] You helped me to open the door—I've got nothin, for you. This is my house. My father's name's Barthwick; he's Member of Parliament—Liberal Member of Parliament: I've told you that before. Have a drink! [*He pours out whisky and drinks it up.*] *I'm* not drunk——[*Subsiding on a sofa.*] Tha's all right. Wha's your name? My name's Barthwick, so's my father's; *I'm* a Liberal too—wha're you?

JONES : [*In a thick, sardonic voice.*] I'm a bloomin' Conservative. My name's Jones! My wife works 'ere; she's the char; she works 'ere.

JACK : Jones? [*He laughs.*] There's 'nother Jones at College with me. I'm not a Socialist myself; I'm a Liberal—there's ve-lill difference, because of the principles of the Lib—Liberal Party. We're all equal before the law—tha's rot, tha's silly. [Laughs.] Wha' was I about to say? Give me some whisky.

[JONES *gives him the whisky he desires, together with a squirt of syphon.*]

Wha' I was goin' tell you was—I've had a row with her. [He waves the reticule.] Have a drink, Jones—sh'd never have got in without you—tha's why I'm giving you a drink. Don' care who knows I've scored her off. Th' cat! [*He throws his feet up on the sofa.*] Don' you make a noise, whatever you do. You pour out a drink—you make yourself good long, long drink—you take cigarette—you take anything you like. Sh'd never have got in without you. [*Closing his eyes.*] You're a Tory—you're a Tory Socialist. I'm Liberal myself—have a drink—I'm an excel'nt chap.

[*His head drops back. He, smiling, falls asleep, and* JONES *stands looking at him; then, snatching up* JACK's *glass, he drinks it off. He picks the reticule from off* JACK's *shirt-front, holds it to the light, and smells at it.*]

JONES : Been on the tiles and brought 'ome some of yer cat's fur. [*He stuffs it into* JACK's *breast pocket.*]

JACK : [*Murmuring.*] I've scored you off! You cat!

[JONES *looks around him furtively; he pours out whisky and drinks it. From the silver box he takes a cigarette, puffs at it, and drinks more whisky. There is no sobriety left in him.*]

JONES : Fat lot o' things they've got 'ere! [*He sees the crimson purse lying on the floor.*] More cat's fur. Puss, puss! [*He fingers it, drops it on the tray, and looks at* JACK.] Calf! Fat calf! [*He sees his own presentment in a mirror. Lifting his hands, with fingers spread, he stares at it; then looks again at* JACK, *clenching his fist as if to batter in his sleeping, smiling face. Suddenly he tilts the rest of the whisky into the glass and drinks it. With cunning glee he takes the silver box and purse and pockets them.*] I'll score *you* off too, that's wot I'll do!

[*He gives a little snarling laugh and lurches to the door. His shoulder rubs against the switch; the light goes out. There is a sound as of a closing outer door.*]

The curtain falls.

The curtain rises again at once.

SCENE II

In the BARTHWICK'S *dining-room.* JACK *is still asleep; the morning light is coming through the curtains. The time is half-past eight.* WHEELER, *brisk person enters with a dust-pan, and* MRS. JONES *more slowly with a scuttle.*

WHEELER : [*Drawing the curtains.*] That precious husband of yours was round for you after you'd gone yesterday, Mrs. Jones. Wanted your money for drink, I suppose. He hangs about the corner here half the time. I saw him outside the "Goat and Bells" when I went to the post last night. If I were you I wouldn't live with him. I wouldn't live with a man that raised his hand to me. I wouldn't put up with it. Why don't you take your children and leave him? If you put up with 'im it'll only make him worse. I never can see why, because a man's married you, he should knock you about.

MRS. JONES : [*Slim, dark-eyed, and dark-haired; oval-faced, and with a smooth, soft, even voice; her manner patient, her way of talking quite impersonal; she wears a blue linen dress, and boots with holes.*] It was nearly two last night before he come home, and he wasn't himself. He made me get up, and he knocked me about; he didn't seem to know *what* he was saying or doing. Of course I *would* leave him, but I'm really afraid of what he'd do to me. He's such a violent man when he's not himself.

WHEELER : Why don't you get him locked up? You'll never have any peace until you get him locked up. If I were you I'd go to the police court tomorrow. That's what I would do.

MRS. JONES : Of course I ought to go, because he does treat me so badly when he's not himself. But you see, Bettina, he has a very hard time—he's been out of work two months, and it preys upon his mind. When he's in work he behaves himself much better. It's when he's out of work that he's so violent.

WHEELER : Well, if you won't take any steps you'll never get rid of him.

MRS. JONES : Of course it's very wearing to me; I don't get my sleep at nights. And it's not as if I were getting help from him, because I have to do for the children and all of us. And he throws such dreadful things up at me, talks of my having men to follow me about. Such a thing never happens; no man ever speaks to me. And of course, it's just the other way. It's what he does that's wrong and makes me so unhappy. And then he's always threatenin' to cut my throat if I leave him. It's all the drink, and things preying on his mind; he's not a bad man really. Sometimes he'll speak quite kind to me, but I've stood so much from him, I don't feel it in me to speak kind back, but just keep myself to myself. And he's all right with the children too, except when he's not himself.

WHEELER : You mean when he's drunk, the beauty.

MRS. JONES : Yes. [*Without change of voice*] There's the young gentleman asleep on the sofa.

[*They both look silently at* JACK.]

MRS. JONES : [*At last, in her soft voice.*] He doesn't look quite himself.

WHEELER : He's a young limb, that's what he is. It's my belief he was tipsy last night, like your husband. It's another kind of bein' out of work that sets him to drink. I'll go and tell Marlow. This is his job.

[*She goes.*]

[MRS. JONES, *upon her knees, begins a gentle sweeping.*]

JACK : [*Waking.*] Who's there? What is it?

MRS. JONES : It's me, sir, Mrs. Jones.

JACK : [*Sitting up and looking round.*] Where is it—what—what time is it?

MRS. JONES : It's getting on for nine o'clock, sir.

JACK : For nine! Why—what! [*Rising, and loosening his tongue; putting hand to his head, and staring hard at* MRS. JONES.] Look here, you, Mrs.—— Mrs. Jones—don't you say you caught me asleep here.

MRS. JONES : No, sir, of course I won't sir.

JACK : It's quite an accident; I don't know how it happened. I must have forgotten to go to bed. It's a queer thing. I've got a most beastly headache. Mind you don't say anything, Mrs. Jones.

[*Goes out and passes* MARLOW *in the doorway.* MARLOW *is young and quiet; he is clean-shaven, and his hair is brushed high from his forehead in a coxcomb. Incidentally a butler, he is first a man. He looks at* MRS. JONES, *and smiles a private smile.*]

MARLOW : Not the first time, and won't be the last. Looked a bit dicky, eh, Mrs. Jones?

MRS. JONES : He didn't look quite himself. Of course I didn't take notice.

MARLOW : You're used to them. How's your old man?

MRS. JONES : [*Softly as throughout.*] Well, he was very bad last night; he didn't seem to know what he was about. He was very late, and he was most abusive. But now, of course, he's asleep.

MARLOW : That's his way of finding a job, eh?

MRS. JONES : As a rule, Mr. Marlow, he goes out early every morning looking for work, and sometimes he comes in fit to drop—and of course I can't say he doesn't try to get it, because he does. Trade's very bad. [*She stands quite still, her fan and brush before her, at the beginning and the end of long vistas of experience, traversing them with her impersonal eye.*] But he's not a good husband to me—last night he hit me, and he was so dreadfully abusive.

MARLOW : Bank 'oliday, eh! He's too fond of the "Goat and Bells," that's what's the matter with him. I see him at the corner late every night. He hangs about.

MRS. JONES : He gets to feeling very low walking about all day after work, and being refused so often, and then when he gets a drop in him it goes to his head. But he shouldn't treat his wife as he treats me. Sometimes I've had to go and walk about at night, when he wouldn't let me stay in the room; but he's sorry for it afterwards. And he hangs about after me, he waits for me in the street; and I don't think he ought to, because I've always been a good wife to him. And I tell him Mrs. Barthwick wouldn't like him coming about the place. But that only makes him angry, and he says dreadful things about the gentry. Of course it was through me that he first lost his place, through his not treating me right; and that's made him bitter against the gentry. He had a very good place as groom in the country; but it made such a stir, because of course he didn't treat me right.

MARLOW : Got the sack?

MRS. JONES : Yes; his employer said he couldn't keep him, because there was a great deal of talk; and he said it was such a bad example. But it's very important for me to keep my work here; I have the three children, and I don't want him to come about after me in the streets, and make a disturbance as he sometimes does.

MARLOW : [*Holding up the empty decanter.*] Not a drain! Next time he hits you get a witness and go down to the court——

MRS. JONES : Yes, I think I've made up my mind. I think I ought to.

MARLOW : That's right. Where's the ciga——?

[*He searches for the silver box; he looks at* MRS. JONES, *who is sweeping on her hands and knees; he checks himself and stands reflecting. From the tray he picks two half-smoked cigarettes, and reads the name on them.*]

Nestor—where the deuce——?

[*With a meditative air he looks again at* MRS. JONES, *and, taking up* JACK's *overcoat, he searches in the pockets.* WHEELER, *with a tray of breakfast things, comes in.*]

MARLOW : [*Aside to* WHEELER.] Have you seen the cigarette-box?

WHEELER : No.

MARLOW : Well, it's gone. I put it on the tray last night. And he's been smoking. [*Showing her the ends of cigarettes.*] It's not in these pockets. He can't have taken it upstairs this morning! Have a good look in his room when he comes down. Who's been in here?

WHEELER : Only me and Mrs. Jones.

MRS. JONES : I've finished here; shall I do the drawing-room now?

WHEELER : [*Looking at her doubtfully.*] Have you seen——Better do the boudwower first.

[MRS. JONES *goes out with pan and brush.* MARLOW *and* WHEELER *look each other in the face.*]

MARLOW : It'll turn up.

WHEELER : [*Hesitating.*] You don't think *she*——
[*Nodding at the door.*]

MARLOW : [*Stoutly.*] I don't——I never believes anything of anybody.

WHEELER : But the master'll have to be told.

MARLOW : You wait a bit, and see if it don't turn up. Suspicion's no business of ours. I set my mind against it.

The curtain falls.

The curtain rises again at once.

SCENE III

BARTHWICK *and* MRS. BARTHWICK *are seated at the breakfast table. He is a man between fifty and sixty; quietly important, with a bald forehead, and pince-nez, and the "Times" in his hand. She is a lady of nearly fifty, well dressed, with greyish hair, good features, and a decided manner. They face each other.*

BARTHWICK : [*From behind his paper.*] The Labour man has got in at the by-election for Barnside, my dear.

MRS. BARTHWICK : Another Labour? I can't think what on earth the country is about.

BARTHWICK : I predicted it. It's not a matter of vast importance.

MRS. BARTHWICK : Not? How can you take it so calmly, John? To me it's simply outrageous. And there you sit, you Liberals, and pretend to encourage these people!

BARTHWICK : [*Frowning.*] The representation of all parties is necessary for any proper reform, for any proper social policy.

MRS. BARTHWICK : I've no patience with your talk of reform—all that nonsense about social policy. We know perfectly well what it is they want; they want things for themselves. Those Socialists and Labour men are an absolutely selfish set of people. They have no sense of patriotism, like the upper classes; *they simply want what we've got.*

BARTHWICK : Want what we've got! [*He stares into space.*] My dear, what are you talking about? [*With a contortion.*] I'm no alarmist.

MRS. BARTHWICK : Cream? Quite uneducated men! Wait until they begin to tax our investments. I'm convinced that when they once get a chance they will tax everything—they've no feeling for the country. You Liberals and Conservatives, you're all alike; you don't see an inch before your noses. You've no imagination, not a scrap of imagination between you. You ought to join hands and nip it in the bud.

BARTHWICK : You're talking nonsense! How is it possible for Liberals and Conservatives to join hands, as you call it? That shows how absurd it is for women——Why, the very essence of a Liberal is to trust in the people!

MRS. BARTHWICK : Now, John, eat your breakfast. As if there were any real difference between you and the Conservatives. All the upper classes have the same interests to protect, and the same principles. [*Calmly.*] Oh! you're sitting upon a volcano, John.

BARTHWICK : What!

MRS. BARTHWICK. I read a letter in the paper yesterday. I forget the man's name, but it made the whole thing perfectly clear. You don't look things in the face.

BARTHWICK : Indeed! [*Heavily.*] I am a Liberal! Drop the subject, please!

MRS. BARTHWICK : Toast? I quite agree with what this man says: Education is simply ruining the lower classes. It unsettles them, and that's the worst thing for us all. I see an enormous difference in the manner of servants.

BARTHWICK : [*With suspicious emphasis.*] I welcome any change that will lead to something better. [*He opens a letter.*] H'm! This is that affair of Master Jack's again. "High Street, Oxford. Sir, We have received Mr. John Barthwick, Senior's, draft for forty pounds!" Oh! the letter's to him! "We now enclose the cheque you cashed with us, which, as we stated in our previous letter, was not met on presentation at your bank. We are, Sir, yours obediently, Moss and Sons, Tailors." H'm! [*Staring at the cheque.*] A pretty business altogether! The boy might have been prosecuted.

MRS. BARTHWICK : Come, John, you know Jack didn't mean anything; he only thought he was overdrawing. I still think his bank ought to have cashed that cheque. They must know your position.

BARTHWICK : [*Replacing in the envelope the letter and the cheque.*] Much good that would have done him in a court of law.

[*He stops as* JACK *comes in, fastening his waistcoat and staunching a razor cut upon his chin.*]

JACK : [*Sitting down between them, and speaking with an artificial joviality.*] Sorry I'm late. [*He looks lugubriously at the dishes.*] Tea, please, mother.

Any letters for me? [BARTHWICK *hands the letter to him.*] But look here, I say, this has been opened! I do wish you wouldn't——

BARTHWICK : [*Touching the envelope.*] I suppose I'm entitled to this name.

JACK : [*Sulkily.*] Well, I can't help having your name, father! [*He reads the letter, and mutters.*] Brutes!

BARTHWICK : [*Eyeing him.*] You don't deserve to be so well out of that.

JACK : Haven't you ragged me enough, dad?

MRS. BARTHWICK : Yes, John, let Jack have his breakfast.

BARTHWICK : If you hadn't had me to come to, where would you have been? It's the merest accident—suppose you had been the son of a poor man or a clerk. Obtaining money with a cheque you knew your bank could not meet. It might have ruined you for life. I can't see what's to become of you if these are your principles. I never did anything of the sort myself.

JACK : I expect you always had lots of money. If you've got plenty of money, of course——

BARTHWICK : On the contrary, I had not your advantages. My father kept me very short of money.

JACK : How much had you, dad?

BARTHWICK : It's not material. The question is, do you feel the gravity of what you did?

JACK : I don't know about the gravity. Of course, I'm very sorry if you think it was wrong. Haven't I said so! I should never have done it at all if I hadn't been so jolly hard up.

BARTHWICK : How much of that forty pounds have you got left, Jack?

JACK : [*Hesitating.*] I don't know—not much.

BARTHWICK : How much?

JACK : [*Desperately.*] I haven't got any.

BARTHWICK. What?

JACK : I know I've got the most beastly headache.

[*He leans his head on his hand.*]

MRS. BARTHWICK : Headache? My dear boy! Can't you eat any breakfast?

JACK : [*Drawing in his breath.*] Too jolly bad!

MRS. BARTHWICK : I'm so sorry. Come with me; dear; I'll give you something that will take it away at once.

[*They leave the room; and* BARTHWICK, *tearing up the letter, goes to the fireplace and puts the pieces in the fire. While he is doing this* MARLOW *comes in, and looking round him, is about quietly to withdraw.*]

BARTHWICK : What's that? What d' you want?

MARLOW : I was looking for Mr. John, sir.

BARTHWICK : What d' you want Mr. John for?

MARLOW : [*With hesitation.*] I thought I should find him here, sir.

BARTHWICK : [*Suspiciously.*] Yes, but what do you want him for?

MARLOW : [*Offhandedly.*] There's a lady called—asked to speak to him for a minute, sir.

BARTHWICK : A lady, at this time in the morning. What sort of a lady?

MARLOW : [*Without expression in his voice.*] I can't tell, sir; no particular sort. She might be after charity. She might be a Sister of Mercy, I should think, sir.

BARTHWICK : Is she dressed like one?

MARLOW : No, sir, she's in plain clothes, sir.

BARTHWICK : Didn't she say what she wanted?

MARLOW : No sir.

BARTHWICK : Where did you leave her?

MARLOW : In the hall, sir.

BARTHWICK : In the hall? How do you know she's not a thief—not got designs on the house?

MARLOW : No, sir, I don't fancy so, sir.

BARTHWICK : Well, show her in here; I'll see her myself.

[MARLOW *goes out with a private gesture of dismay. He soon returns, ushering in a young pale lady with dark eyes and pretty figure, in a modish, black, but rather shabby dress, a black and white trimmed hat with a bunch of Parma violets wrongly placed, and fuzzy-spotted veil. At the sight of* MR. BARTHWICK *she exhibits every sign of nervousness.* MARLOW *goes out.*]

UNKNOWN LADY : Oh! but—I beg pardon there's some mistake—I [*She turns to fly.*]

BARTHWICK : Whom did you want to see, madam?

UNKNOWN : [*Stopping and looking back.*] It was Mr. *John* Barthwick I wanted to see.

BARTHWICK : I am John Barthwick, madam. What can I have the pleasure of doing for you?

UNKNOWN : Oh! I—I don't [*She drops her eyes.* BARTHWICK *scrutinises her, and purses his lips.*]

BARTHWICK : It was my son, perhaps, you wished to see?

UNKNOWN : [*Quickly.*] Yes, of course, it's your son.

BARTHWICK : May I ask whom I have the pleasure of speaking to?

UNKNOWN : [*Appeal and hardiness upon her face.*] My name is——oh! it doesn't matter—I don't want to make any fuss. I just want to see your son for a minute. [*Boldly.*] In fact, I *must* see him.

BARTHWICK : [*Controlling his uneasiness.*] My son is not very well. If necessary, no doubt I could attend to the matter; be so kind as to let me know——

UNKNOWN : Oh! but I *must* see him—I've come on purpose—[*She bursts out nervously.*] I don't want to make any fuss, but the fact is, last—last night your son took away—he took away my [*She stops.*]

BARTHWICK : [*Severely.*] Yes, madam, what?

UNKNOWN : He took away my—my reticule.

BARTHWICK : Your reti——?

UNKNOWN : I don't care about the reticule; it's not *that* I want—I'm sure I don't want to make any fuss—[*her face is quivering*]—but —but—all my money was in it!

BARTHWICK : In what—in what?

UNKNOWN : In my purse, in the reticule. It was a crimson silk purse. Really, I wouldn't have come—I don't want to make any fuss. But I must get my money back—mustn't I?

BARTHWICK : Do you tell me that my son——?

UNKNOWN : Oh! well, you see, he wasn't quite—I mean he was——[*She smiles mesmerically.*]

BARTHWICK : I beg your pardon.

UNKNOWN : [*Stamping her foot.*] Oh! don't you see—tipsy! We had a quarrel.

BARTHWICK : [*Scandalised.*] How? Where?

UNKNOWN : [*Defiantly.*] At my place. We'd had supper at the——and your son——

BARTHWICK : [*Pressing the bell.*] May I ask how you knew this house? Did he give you his name and address?

UNKNOWN : [*Glancing sidelong.*] I got it out of his overcoat.

BARTHWICK : [*Sardonically.*] Oh! you got it out of his overcoat. And may I ask if my son will know you by daylight?

UNKNOWN : Know me? I should jolly—I mean, of course he will!

[MARLOW *comes in.*]

BARTHWICK : Ask Mr. John to come down.

[MARLOW *goes out, and* BARTHWICK *walks uneasily about.*]

And how long have you enjoyed his acquaintanceship?

UNKNOWN : Only since—only since Good Friday.

BARTHWICK : I am at a loss—I repeat I am at a loss——

[*He glances at this unknown lady, who stands with eyes cast down, twisting her hands. And suddenly* JACK *appears. He stops on seeing who is here, and the unknown lady hysterically giggles. There is a silence.*]

BARTHWICK : [*Portentously.*] This young—er—lady says that last night—I think you said last night madam—you took away——

UNKNOWN : [*Impulsively.*] My reticule, and all my money was in a crimson silk purse.

JACK : Reticule [*Looking round for any chance to get away.*] I don't know anything about it.

BARTHWICK : [*Sharply.*] Come, do you deny seeing this young lady last night?

JACK : Deny? No, of course. [*Whispering.*] Why did you give me away like this? What on earth did you come here for?

UNKNOWN : [*Tearfully.*] I'm sure I didn't want to—it's not likely, is it? You snatched it out of my hand—you know you did—and the purse had all my money in it. I didn't follow you last night because I didn't want to make a fuss and it was so late, and you were so——

BARTHWICK : Come, sir, don't turn your back on me—explain!

JACK : [*Desperately.*] I don't remember anything about it. [*In a low voice to his friend.*] Why on earth couldn't you have written?

UNKNOWN : [*Sullenly.*] I want it now; I must have, it—I've got to pay my rent to-day. [*She looks at* BARTHWICK.] They're only too glad to jump on people who are not—not *well off.*

JACK : I don't remember anything about it, really. I don't remember anything about last night at all. [*He puts his hand up to his head.*] It's all—cloudy, and I've got such a beastly headache.

UNKNOWN : But you *took* it; you know you did. You said you'd score me off.

JACK : Well, then, it must be here. I remember now—I remember something. Why did I take the beastly thing?

BARTHWICK : Yes, why did you take the beastly——
[*He turns abruptly to the window.*]

UNKNOWN : [*With her mesmeric smile.*] You weren't quite were you?

JACK : [*Smiling pallidly.*] I'm *awfully* sorry. If there's anything I can do——

BARTHWICK : Do? You can restore this property, I suppose.

JACK. I'll go and have a look, but I really don't think I've got it.

[*He goes out hurriedly. And* BARTHWICK, *placing a chair, motions to the visitor to sit; then, with pursed lips, he stands and eyes her fixedly. She sits, and steals a look at him; then turns away, and, drawing up her veil, stealthily wipes her eyes. And* JACK *comes back.*]

JACK : [*Ruefully holding out the empty reticule.*] Is that the thing? I've looked all over—I can't find the purse anywhere. Are you sure it was there?

UNKNOWN : [*Tearfully.*] Sure? Of course I'm sure. A crimson silk purse. It was all the money I had.

JACK : I really am awfully sorry—my head's so jolly bad. I've asked the butler, but he hasn't seen it.

UNKNOWN : I *must* have my money——

JACK : Oh! Of course—that'll be all right; I'll see that that's all right. How much?

UNKNOWN : [*Sullenly.*] Seven pounds—twelve—it's all I've got in the world.

JACK : That'll be all right; I'll—send you a—cheque.

UNKNOWN : [*Eagerly.*] No; now, please. Give me what was in my purse; I've got to pay my rent this morning. They won't' give me another day; I'm a fortnight behind already.

JACK : [*Blankly.*] I'm awfully sorry; I really haven't a penny in my pocket.

[*He glances stealthily at* BARTHWICK.]

UNKNOWN : [*Excitedly.*] Come I say you must—it's my money, and you took it. I'm not going away without it. They'll turn me out of my place.

JACK : [*Clasping his head.*] But I can't give you what I haven't got. Don't I tell you I haven't a beastly cent.

UNKNOWN : [*Tearing at her handkerchief.*] Oh! do give it me! [*She puts her hands together in appeal; then, with sudden fierceness.*] If you don't I'll summons you. It's stealing, that's what it is!

BARTHWICK : [*Uneasily.*] One moment, please. As a matter of—-er —principle, I shall settle this claim. [*He produces money.*] Here is eight pounds; the extra will cover the value of the purse and your cab fares. I need make no comment—no thanks are necessary.

[*Touching the bell, he holds the door ajar in silence. The unknown lady stores the money in her reticule, she looks from* JACK *to* BARTHWICK, *and her face is quivering faintly with a smile. She hides it with her hand, and steals away. Behind her* BARTHWICK *shuts the door.*]

BARTHWICK : [*With solemnity.*] H'm! This is nice thing to happen!

JACK : [*Impersonally.*] What awful luck!

BARTHWICK : So this is the way that forty pounds has gone! One thing after another! Once more I should like to know where you'd have been if it hadn't been for me! You don't seem to have any principles. You—you're one of those who are a nuisance to society; you—you're dangerous! What your mother would say I don't know. Your conduct, as far as I can see, is absolutely unjustifiable. It's—it's criminal. Why, a poor man who behaved as you've done —d' you think he'd have any mercy shown him? What you want is a good lesson. You and your sort are—[*he speaks with feeling*]—a nuisance to the community. Don't ask me to help you next time. You're not fit to be helped.

JACK : [*Turning upon his sire, with unexpected fierceness.*] All right, I won't then, and see how you like it. You wouldn't have helped me this time, I know, if you hadn't been scared the thing would get into the papers. Where are the cigarettes?

BARTHWICK : [*Regarding him uneasily.*] Well I'll say no more about it. [*He rings the bell.*] I'll pass it over for this once, but—— [MARLOW *comes in.*] You can clear away.

[*He hides his face behind the "Times."*]

JACK : [*Brightening.*] I say, Marlow, where are the cigarettes?

MARLOW : I put the box out with the whisky last night, sir, but this morning I can't find it anywhere.

JACK : Did you look in my room?

MARLOW : Yes, sir; I've looked all over the house. I found two Nestor ends in the tray this morning, so you must have been smokin' last night, sir. [*Hesitating.*] I'm really afraid some one's purloined the box.

JACK : [*Uneasily.*] Stolen it!

BARTHWICK : What's that? The cigarette-box! Is anything else missing?

MARLOW : No, sir; I've been through the plate.

BARTHWICK : Was the house all right this morning? None of the windows open?

MARLOW : No, sir. [*Quietly to* JACK.] You left your latch-key in the door last night, sir.

[*He hands it back, unseen by* BARTHWICK]

JACK : Tst!

BARTHWICK : Who's been in the room this morning?

MARLOW : Me and Wheeler, and Mrs. Jones is all, sir, as far as I know.

BARTHWICK : Have you asked Mrs. Barthwick?

[*To* JACK.] Go and ask your mother if she's had it; ask her to look and see if she's missed anything else.

[JACK *goes upon this mission.*]

Nothing is more disquieting than losing things like this.

MARLOW : No, sir.

BARTHWICK : Have you any suspicions?

MARLOW : No, sir.

BARTHWICK : This Mrs. Jones—how long has she been working here?

MARLOW : Only this last month, sir.

BARTHWICK : What sort of person?

MARLOW : I don't know much about her, sir; seems a very quiet, respectable woman.

BARTHWICK : Who did the room this morning?

MARLOW : Wheeler and Mrs. Jones, Sir.

BARTHWICK : [*With his forefinger upraised.*] Now, was this Mrs. Jones in the room alone at any time?

MARLOW : [*Expressionless.*] Yes, Sir.

BARTHWICK : How do you know that?

MARLOW : [*Reluctantly.*] I found her here, sir.

BARTHWICK : And has Wheeler been in the room alone?

MARLOW : No, sir, she's not, sir. I should say, sir, that Mrs. Jones seems a very honest——

BARTHWICK : [*Holding up his hand.*] I want to know this: Has this Mrs. Jones been here the whole morning?

MARLOW : Yes, sir—no, sir—she stepped over to the greengrocer's for cook.

BARTHWICK : H'm! Is she in the house now?

MARLOW : Yes, sir.

BARTHWICK. Very good. I shall make a point of clearing this up. On principle I shall make a point of fixing the responsibility; it goes to the foundations of security. In all your interests——

MARLOW : Yes, sir.

BARTHWICK : What sort of circumstances is this Mrs. Jones in? Is her husband in work?

MARLOW : I believe not, sir.

BARTHWICK : Very well. Say nothing about it to any one. Tell Wheeler not to speak of it, and ask Mrs. Jones to step up here.

MARLOW : Very good, sir.

[MARLOW *goes out, his face concerned; and* BARTHWICK *stays, his face judicial and a little pleased, as befits a man conducting an inquiry.* MRS. BARTHWICK *and her son come in.*]

BARTHWICK : Well, my dear, you've not seen it, I suppose?

MRS. BARTHWICK : No. But what an extraordinary thing, John! Marlow, of course, is out of the question. I'm certain none of the maids as for cook!

BARTHWICK : Oh, cook!

MRS. BARTHWICK : Of course! It's perfectly detestable to me to suspect anybody.

BARTHWICK : It is not a question of one's feelings. It's a question of justice. On principle——

MRS. BARTHWICK : I shouldn't be a bit surprised if the charwoman knew something about it. It was Laura who recommended her.

BARTHWICK : [*Judicially.*] I am going to have Mrs. Jones up. Leave it to me; and—er—remember that nobody is guilty until they're proved so. I shall be careful. I have no intention of frightening her; I shall give her every chance. I hear she's in poor circumstances. If we are not able to do much for them we are bound to have the greatest sympathy with the poor. [MRS. JONES *comes in.*] [*Pleasantly.*] Oh! good morning, Mrs. Jones.

MRS. JONES : [*Soft, and even, unemphatic.*] Good morning, sir! Good morning, ma'am!

BARTHWICK : About your husband—he's not in work, I hear?

MRS. JONES : No, sir; of course he's not in work just now.

BARTHWICK : Then I suppose he's earning nothing.

MRS. JONES : No, sir, he's not earning anything just now, sir.

BARTHWICK : And how many children have you?

MRS. JONES : Three children; but of course they don't eat very much sir. [*A little silence.*]

BARTHWICK : And how old is the eldest?

MRS. JONES : Nine years old, sir.

BARTHWICK : Do they go to school?

MRS. JONES : Yes, sir, they all three go to school every day.

BARTHWICK : [*Severely.*] And what about their food when you're out at work?

MRS. JONES : Well, sir, I have to give them their dinner to take with them. Of course I'm not always able to give them anything; sometimes I have to send them without; but my husband is very good about the children when he's in work. But when he's not in work of course he's a very difficult man.

BARTHWICK : He drinks, I suppose?

MRS. JONES : Yes, sir. Of course I can't say he doesn't drink, because he does.

BARTHWICK : And I suppose he takes all your money?

MRS. JONES : No, sir, he's very good about my money, except when he's not himself, and then, of course, he treats me very badly.

BARTHWICK : Now what is he—your husband?

MRS. JONES : By profession, sir, of course he's a groom.

BARTHWICK : A groom! How came he to lose his place?

MRS. JONES : He lost his place a long time ago, sir,

and he's never had a very long job since; and now, of course, the motor-cars are against him.

BARTHWICK : When were you married to him, Mrs. Jones?

MRS. JONES : Eight years ago, sir—that was in——

MRS. BARTHWICK : [*Sharply.*] Eight? You said the eldest child was nine.

MRS. JONES : Yes, ma'am; of course that was why he lost his place. He didn't treat me rightly, and of course his employer said he couldn't keep him because of the example.

BARTHWICK : You mean he—ahem——

MRS. JONES : Yes, sir; and of course after he lost his place he married me.

MRS. BARTHWICK : You actually mean to say you—you were——

BARTHWICK : My dear——

MRS. BARTHWICK : [*Indignantly.*] How disgraceful!

BARTHWICK : [*Hurriedly.*] And where are you living now, Mrs. Jones?

MRS. JONES : We've not got a home, sir. Of course we've been obliged to put away most of our things.

BARTHWICK : Put your things away! You mean to—to—er—to pawn them?

MRS. JONES : Yes, sir, to put them away. We're living in Merthyr Street—that is close by here, sir—at No. 34. We just have the one room.

BARTHWICK : And what do you pay a week?

MRS. JONES : We pay six shillings a week, sir, for a furnished room.

BARTHWICK : And I suppose you're behind in the rent?

MRS. JONES : Yes, sir, we're a little behind in the rent.

BARTHWICK : But *you're* in good work, aren't you?

MRS. JONES : Well, sir, I have a day in Stamford Place Thursdays. And Mondays and Wednesdays and Fridays I come here. But to-day, of course, is a half-day, because of yesterday's Bank Holiday.

BARTHWICK : I see; four days a week, and you get half a crown a day, is that it?

MRS. JONES : Yes, sir, and my dinner; but sometimes it's only half a day, and that's eighteen pence.

BARTHWICK : And when your husband earns anything he spends it in drink, I suppose?

MRS. JONES : Sometimes he does, sir, and sometimes he gives it to me for the children. Of course he would work if he could get it, sir, but it seems there are a great many people out of work.

BARTHWICK : Ah! Yes. We—er—won't go into that. [*Sympathetically.*] And how about your work here? Do you find it hard?

MRS. JONES : Oh! no, sir, not very hard, sir; except of course, when I don't get my sleep at night.

BARTHWICK : Ah! And you help do all the rooms? And sometimes, I suppose, you go out for cook?

MRS. JONES : Yes, Sir.

BARTHWICK : And you've been out this morning?

MRS. JONES : Yes, sir, of course I had to go to the greengrocer's.

BARTHWICK : Exactly. So your husband earns nothing? And he's a bad character.

MRS. JONES : No, sir, I don't say that, sir. I think there's a great deal of good in him; though he does treat me very bad sometimes. And of course I don't like to leave him, but I think I ought to, because really I hardly know how to stay with him. He often raises his hand to me. Not long ago he gave me a blow here [*touches her breast*] and I can feel it now. So I think I ought to leave him, don't *you*, sir?

BARTHWICK : Ah! I can't help you there. It's a very serious thing to leave your husband. Very serious thing.

MRS. JONES : Yes, sir, of course I'm afraid of what he might do to me if I were to leave him; he can be so very violent.

BARTHWICK : H'm! Well, that I can't pretend to say anything about. It's the bad principle I'm speaking of——

MRS. JONES : Yes, sir; I know nobody can help me. I know I must decide for myself, and of course I know that he has a very hard life. And he's fond of the children, and it's very hard for him to see them going without food.

BARTHWICK : [*Hastily.*] Well—er—thank you, I just wanted to hear about you. I don't think I need detain you any longer, Mrs.—Jones.

MRS. JONES : No, sir, thank you, sir.

BARTHWICK : Good morning, then.

MRS. JONES : Good morning, sir; good morning, ma'am.

BARTHWICK : [*Exchanging glances with his wife.*] By the way, Mrs. Jones—I think it is only fair to tell you, a silver cigarette-box —er—is missing.

MRS. JONES : [*Looking from one face to the other.*] I am very sorry, sir.

BARTHWICK : Yes; you have not seen it, I suppose?

MRS. JONES : [*Realising that suspicion is upon her;*

JONES : What you back so soon for?

MRS. JONES : I only had the half day to-day, Jem.

JONES : [*On his back, and in a drowsy voice.*] Got anything for dinner?

MRS. JONES : Mrs. Barthwick's cook gave me a little bit of bacon. I'm going to make a stew. [*She prepares for cooking.*] There's fourteen shillings owing for rent, James, and of course I've only got two and fourpence. They'll be coming for it to-day.

JONES : [*Turning towards her on his elbow.*] Let 'em come and find my surprise packet. I've had enough o' this tryin' for work. Why should I go round and round after a job like a bloomin' squirrel in a cage. "Give us a job, sir"—"Take a man on"—"Got a wife and three children." Sick of it I am! I'd sooner lie here and rot. "Jones, you come and join the demonstration; come and 'old a flag, and listen to the ruddy orators, and go 'ome as empty as you came." There's some that seems to like *that*—the sheep! When I go seekin' for a job now, and see the brutes lookin' me up an' down, it's like a thousand serpents in me. I'm not arskin' for any treat. A man wants to sweat hisself silly and not allowed—that's a rum start, ain't it? A man wants to sweat his soul out to keep the breath in him and ain't allowed—that's justice—that's freedom and all the rest of it! [*He turns his face towards the wall.*] You're so milky mild; you don't know what goes on inside o' me. I'm done with the silly game. If they want me, let 'em come for me!

[MRS. JONES *stops cooking and stands unmoving at the table.*]

I've tried and done with it, I tell you. I've never been afraid of what's before *me.* You mark my words—if you think they've broke my spirit, you're mistook. I'll lie and rot sooner than arsk 'em again. What makes you stand like that—you long-sufferin', Gawd-forsaken image—that's why I can't keep my hands off you. So now you know. Work! You can work, but you haven't the spirit of a louse!

MRS. JONES : [*Quietly.*] You talk more wild sometimes when you're yourself, James, than when you're not. If you don't get work, how are we to go on? They won't let us stay here; they're looking to their money to-day, I know.

JONES : I see this Barthwick's o' yours every day goin' down to Pawlyment snug and comfortable to talk his silly soul out; an' I see that young calf, his son, swellin' it about, and goin' on the razzle-dazzle. Wot 'ave they done that makes 'em any better than wot I am? They never did a day's work in their lives. I see 'em day after day——

MRS. JONES : And I wish you wouldn't come after me like that, and hang about the house. You don't seem able to keep away at all, and whatever you do it for I can't think, because of course they notice it.

JONES : I suppose I may go where I like. Where *may* I go? The other day I went to a place in the Edgware Road. "Gov'nor," I says to the boss, "take me on," I says. "I 'aven't done a stroke o' work not these two months; it takes the heart out of a man," I says; "I'm one to work; I'm not afraid of anything you can give me!" "My good man," 'e says, "I've had thirty of you here this morning. I took the first two," he says, "and that's all I want." "Thank you, then rot the world!" I says. "Blasphemin'," he says, "is not the way to get a job. Out you go, my lad!" [*He laughs sardonically.*] Don't you raise your voice because you're starvin'; don't yer even think of it; take it lyin' down! Take it like a sensible man, carn't you? And a little way down the street a lady says to me: [*Pinching his voice*] "D' you want to earn a few pence, my man?" and gives me her dog to 'old outside a shop—fat as a butler 'e was—tons o' meat had gone to the makin' of *him*. It did 'er good, it did, made 'er feel 'erself that *charitable*, but I see 'er lookin' at the copper standin' alongside o' me, for fear I should make off with 'er bloomin' fat dog. [*He sits on the edge of the bed and puts a boot on. Then looking up.*] What's in that head o' yours? [*Almost pathetically.*] Carn't you speak for once?

[*There is a knock, and* MRS. SEDDON, *the landlady, appears, an anxious, harassed, shabby woman in working clothes.*]

MRS. SEDDON : I thought I 'eard you come in, Mrs. Jones. I've spoke to my 'usband, but he says he really can't afford to wait another day.

JONES : [*With scowling jocularity.*] Never you mind what your 'usband says, you go your own way like a proper independent woman. Here, Jenny, chuck her that.

[*Producing a sovereign from his trousers pocket, he throws it to his wife, who catches it in her apron with a gasp.* JONES *resumes the lacing of his boots.*]

MRS. JONES : [*Rubbing the sovereign stealthily.*] I'm very sorry we're so late with it, and of course it's fourteen shillings, so if you've got six that will be right.

[MRS. SEDDON *takes the sovereign and fumbles for the change.*]

JONES : [*With his eyes fixed on his boots.*] Bit of a surprise for yer, ain't it?

MRS. SEDDON : Thank you, and I'm sure I'm very much obliged. [*She does indeed appear surprised.*] I'll bring you the change.

JONES : [*Mockingly.*] Don't mention it.

MRS. SEDDON : Thank you, and I'm sure I'm very much obliged. [*She slides away.*]

[MRS. JONES *gazes at* JONES *who is still lacing up his boots.*]

JONES : I've had a bit of luck. [*Pulling out the crimson purse and some loose coins.*] Picked up a purse— seven pound and more.

MRS. JONES : Oh, James!

JONES : Oh, James! What about Oh, James! I picked it up I tell you. This is lost property, this is!

MRS. JONES : But isn't there a name in it, or something?

JONES : Name? No, there ain't no name. This don't belong to such as 'ave visitin' cards. This belongs to a perfec' lidy. Tike an' smell it. [*He pitches her the purse, which she puts gently to her nose.*] Now, you tell me what I ought to have done. You tell me that. You can always tell me what I ought to ha' done, can't yer?

MRS. JONES : [*Laying down the purse.*] I can't say what you ought to have done, James. Of course the money wasn't yours; you've taken somebody else's money.

JONES : Finding's keeping. I'll take it as wages for the time I've gone about the streets asking for what's my rights. I'll take it for what's *overdue,* d' ye hear? [*With strange triumph.*] I've got money in my pocket, my girl.

[MRS. JONES *goes on again with the preparation of the meal,* JONES *looking at her furtively.*]

Money in my pocket! And I'm not goin' to waste it. With this 'ere money I'm goin' to Canada. I'll let you have a pound. [*A silence.*] You've often talked of leavin' me. You've often told me I treat you badly—well I 'ope you'll be glad when I'm gone.

MRS. JONES : [*Impassively.*] You *have,* treated me very badly, James, and of course I can't prevent your going; but I can't tell whether I shall be glad when you're gone.

JONES : It'll change my luck. I've 'ad nothing but bad luck since I first took up with you. [*More softly.*] And you've 'ad no bloomin' picnic.

MRS. JONES : Of course it would have been better

for us if we had never met. We weren't meant for each other. But you're set against me, that's what you are, and you *have* been for a long time. And you treat me so badly, James, going after that Rosie and all. You don't ever seem to think of the children that I've had to bring into the world, and of all the trouble I've had to keep them, and what'll become of them when you're gone.

JONES : [*Crossing the room gloomily.*] If you think I want to leave the little beggars you're bloomin' well mistaken.

MRS. JONES : Of course I know you're fond of them.

JONES : [*Fingering the purse, half angrily.*] Well, then, you stow it, old girl. The kids'll get along better with you than when I'm here. If I'd ha' known as much as I do now, I'd never ha' had one o' them. What's the use o' bringin' 'em into a state o' things like this? It's a crime, that's what it is; but you find it out too late; that's what's the matter with this 'ere world.

[*He puts the purse back in his pocket.*]

MRS. JONES : Of course it would have been better for them, poor little things; but they're your own children, and I wonder at you talkin' like that. I should miss them dreadfully if I was to lose them.

JONES : [*Sullenly.*] An' you ain't the only one. If I make money out there—[*Looking up, he sees her shaking out his coat—in a changed voice.*] Leave that coat alone!

[*The silver box drops from the pocket, scattering the cigarettes upon the bed. Taking up the box she stares at it; he rushes at her and snatches the box away.*]

MRS. JONES : [*Cowering back against the bed.*] Oh, Jem! oh, Jem!

JONES : [*Dropping the box onto the table.*] You mind what you're sayin'! When I go out I'll take and chuck it in the water along with that there purse. I 'ad it when I was in liquor, and for what you do when you're in liquor you're not responsible—and that's Gawd's truth as you ought to know. I don't want the thing—I won't have it. I took it out o' spite. I'm no thief, I tell you; and don't you call me one, or it'll be the worse for you.

MRS. JONES : [*Twisting her apron strings.*] It's Mr. Barthwick's! You've taken away my reputation. Oh, Jem, whatever made you?

JONES : What d' you mean?

MRS. JONES : It's been missed; they think it's me. Oh! whatever made you do it, Jem?

JONES : I tell you I was in liquor. I don't want it; what's the good of it to me? If I were to pawn it they'd only nab me. I'm no thief. I'm no worse than wot that young Barthwick is; he brought 'ome that purse that I picked up—a lady's purse—'ad it off 'er in a row, kept sayin' 'e'd scored 'er off. Well, I scored 'im off. Tight as an owl 'e was! And d' you think anything'll happen to him?

MRS. JONES : [*As though speaking to herself.*] Oh, Jem! it's the bread out of our mouths!

JONES : Is it then? I'll make it hot for 'em yet. What about that purse? What about young BARTHWICK?

[MRS. JONES *comes forward to the table and tries to take the box;* JONES *prevents her.*] What do you want with that? You drop it, I say!

MRS. JONES : I'll take it back and tell them all about it. [*She attempts to wrest the box from him.*]

JONES : Ah, would yer?

[*He drops the box, and rushes on her with a snarl. She slips back past the bed. He follows; a chair is overturned. The door is opened;* SNOW *comes in, a detective in plain clothes and bowler hat, with clipped moustaches.* JONES *drops his arms,* MRS. JONES *stands by the window gasping;* SNOW, *advancing swiftly to the table, puts his hand on the silver box.*]

SNOW : Doin' a bit o' skylarkin'? Fancy this is what I'm after. J. B., the very same. [*He gets back to the door, scrutinising the crest and cypher on the box. To* MRS. JONES.] I'm a police officer. Are you Mrs. Jones?

MRS. JONES : Yes, sir.

SNOW : My instructions are to take you on a charge of stealing this box from J. BARTHWICK, Esquire, M.P., of 6, Rockingham Gate. Anything you say may be used against you. Well, Missis?

MRS. JONES : [*In her quiet voice, still out of breath, her hand upon her breast.*] Of course I did *not* take it, sir. I never have taken anything that didn't belong to me; and of course I know nothing about it.

SNOW : You were at the house this morning; you did the room in which the box was left; you were alone in the room. I find the box 'ere. You say you didn't take it?

MRS. JONES : Yes, sir, of course I say I did not take it, because I did *not.*

SNOW : Then how does the box come to be here?

MRS. JONES : I would rather not say anything about it.

SNOW : Is this your husband?

MRS. JONES : Yes, sir, this is my husband, sir.

SNOW : Do you wish to say anything before I take her?

[JONES *remains silent, with his head bent down.*]

Well then, Missis. I'll just trouble you to come along with me quietly.

MRS. JONES : [*Twisting her hands.*] Of course I wouldn't say I hadn't taken it if I had—and I *didn't* take it, indeed I didn't. Of course I know appearances are against me, and I *can't* tell you what really happened: But my children are at school, and they'll be coming home—and I don't know what they'll do without me.

SNOW : Your 'usband'll see to them, don't you worry. [*He takes the woman gently by the arm.*]

JONES : You drop it—she's all right! [*Sullenly.*] I took the thing myself.

SNOW : [*Eyeing him*] There, there, it does you credit. Come along, Missis.

JONES : [*Passionately.*] Drop it, I say, you blooming teck. She's my wife; she's a respectable woman. Take her if you dare!

SNOW. Now, now. What's the good of this? Keep a civil tongue, and it'll be the better for all of us.

[*He puts his whistle in his mouth and draws the woman to the door.*]

JONES : [*With a rush.*] Drop her, and put up your 'ands, or I'll soon make yer. You leave her alone, will yer! Don't I tell yer, I took the thing myself.

SNOW : [*Blowing his whistle.*] Drop your hands, or I'll take you too. Ah, would you?

[JONES, *closing, deals him a blow. A Policeman in uniform appears; there is a short struggle and* JONES *is overpowered.* MRS. JONES *raises her hands and drops her face on them.*]

The curtain falls.

SCENE II

The BARTHWICKS' *dining-room the same evening. The* BARTHWICKS *are seated at dessert.*

MRS. BARTHWICK : John! [*A silence broken by the cracking of nuts.*] John!

BARTHWICK : I wish you'd speak about the nuts—they're uneatable. [*He puts one in his mouth.*]

MRS. BARTHWICK : It's not the season for them. I called on the Holyroods.

[BARTHWICK *fills his glass with port.*]

JACK : Crackers, please, Dad.

[BARTHWICK *passes the crackers. His demeanour is reflective.*]

MRS. BARTHWICK : Lady Holyrood has got very stout. I've noticed it coming for a long time.

BARTHWICK : [*Gloomily.*] Stout? [*He takes up the crackers—with transparent airiness.*] The Holyroods had some trouble with their servants, hadn't they?

JACK : Crackers, please, Dad.

BARTHWICK : [*Passing the crackers.*] It got into the papers. The cook, wasn't it?

MRS. BARTHWICK : No, the lady's maid. I was talking it over with Lady Holyrood. The girl used to have her young man to see her.

BARTHWICK : [*Uneasily.*] I'm not sure they were wise——

MRS. BARTHWICK : My dear John, what are you talking about? How could there be any alternative? Think of the effect on the other servants!

BARTHWICK : Of course in principle—I wasn't thinking of that.

JACK : [*Maliciously.*] Crackers, please, Dad.

[BARTHWICK *is compelled to pass the crackers.*]

MRS. BARTHWICK : Lady Holyrood told me: "I had her up," she said; "I said to her, 'You'll leave my house at once; I think your conduct disgraceful. I can't tell, I don't know, and I don't wish to know, what you were doing. I send you away on principle; you need not come to me for a character.' And the girl said: 'If you don't give me my notice, my lady, I want a month's wages. I'm perfectly respectable. I've done nothing.'"—Done nothing!

BARTHWICK : H'm!

MRS. BARTHWICK : Servants have too much license. They hang together so terribly you never can tell what they're really thinking; it's as if they were all in a conspiracy to keep you in the dark. Even with Marlow, you feel that he never lets you know what's really in his mind. I hate that secretiveness; it destroys all confidence. I feel sometimes I should like to shake him.

JACK : Marlow's a most decent chap. It's simply beastly every one knowing your affairs.

BARTHWICK : The less you say about that the better!

MRS. BARTHWICK : It goes all through the lower classes. You can *not* tell when they are speaking the truth. To-day when I was shopping after leaving the Holyroods, one of these unemployed came up and spoke to me. I suppose I only had twenty yards or so to walk to the carnage, but he seemed to spring up in the street.

BARTHWICK : Ah! You must be very careful whom you speak to in these days.

MRS. BARTHWICK : I didn't answer him, of course. But I could see at once that he wasn't telling the truth.

BARTHWICK : [*Cracking a nut.*] There's one very good rule—look at their eyes.

JACK : Crackers, please, Dad.

BARTHWICK : [*Passing the crackers.*] If their eyes are straightforward I sometimes give them sixpence. It's against my principles, but it's most difficult to refuse. If you see that they're desperate, and dull, and shifty-looking, as so many of them are, it's certain to mean drink, or crime, or something unsatisfactory.

MRS. BARTHWICK : This man had dreadful eyes. He looked as if he could commit a murder. "I've 'ad nothing to eat to-day," he said. Just like that.

BARTHWICK : What was William about? He ought to have been waiting.

JACK : [*Raising his wine-glass to his nose.*] Is this the '63, Dad?

[BARTHWICK, *holding his wine-glass to his eye, lowers it and passes it before his nose.*]

MRS. BARTHWICK : I hate people that can't speak the truth. [*Father and son exchange a look behind their port.*] It's just as easy to speak the truth as not. *I've* always found it easy enough. It makes it impossible to tell what is genuine; one feels as if one were continually being taken in.

BARTHWICK : [*Sententiously.*] The lower classes are their own enemies. If they would only trust us, they would get on so much better.

MRS. BARTHWICK : But even then it's so often their own fault. Look at that Mrs. Jones this morning.

BARTHWICK : I only want to do what's right in that matter. I had occasion to see Roper this afternoon. I mentioned it to him. He's coming in this evening. It all depends on what the detective says. I've had my doubts. I've been thinking it over.

MRS. BARTHWICK : The woman impressed me most unfavourably. She seemed to have no shame. That affair she was talking about—she and the man when they were young, so immoral! And before you and Jack! I could have put her out of the room!

BARTHWICK : Oh! I don't want to excuse them, but in looking at these matters one must consider——

MRS. BARTHWICK : Perhaps you'll say the man's employer was wrong in dismissing him?

BARTHWICK : Of course not. It's not there that I feel doubt. What I ask myself is——

JACK : Port, please, Dad.

BARTHWICK : [*Circulating the decanter in religious imitation of the rising and setting of the sun.*] I ask myself whether we are sufficiently careful in making inquiries about people before we engage them, especially as regards moral conduct.

JACK : Pass the port, please, Mother!

MRS. BARTHWICK : [*Passing it.*] My dear boy, aren't you drinking too much?

[JACK *fills his glass.*]

MARLOW : [*Entering.*] Detective Snow to see you, sir.

BARTHWICK : [*Uneasily.*] Ah! say I'll be with him in a minute.

MRS. BARTHWICK : [*Without turning.*] Let him come in here, Marlow.

[SNOW *enters in an overcoat, his bowler hat in hand.*]

BARTHWICK : [*Half-rising.*] Oh! Good evening!

SNOW : Good evening, sir; good evening, ma'am. I've

called round to report what I've done, rather late, I'm afraid—another case took me away. [*He takes the silver box out of his pocket, causing a sensation in the* BARTHWICK *family.*] This is the identical article, I believe.

BARTHWICK : Certainly, certainly.

SNOW : Havin' your crest and cypher, as you described to me, sir, I'd no hesitation in the matter.

BARTHWICK : Excellent. Will you have a glass of [*he glances at the waning port*]—er—sherry—[*pours out sherry*]. Jack, just give Mr. Snow this.

[JACK *rises and gives the glass to* SNOW; *then, lolling in his chair, regards him indolently.*]

SNOW : [*Drinking off wine and putting down the glass.*] After seeing you I went round to this woman's lodgings, sir. It's a low neighborhood, and I thought it as well to place a constable below—and not without 'e was wanted, as things turned out.

BARTHWICK : Indeed!

SNOW : Yes, sir, I'ad some trouble. I asked her to account for the presence of the article. She could give me no answer, except to deny the theft; so I took her into custody; then her husband came for me, so I was obliged to take him, too, for assault. He was very violent on the way to the station—very violent—threatened you and your son, and altogether he was a handful, I can till you.

MRS. BARTHWICK : What a ruffian he must be!

SNOW : Yes, ma'am, a rough customer.

JACK : [*Sipping his wine, bemused.*] Punch the beggar's head.

SNOW : Given to drink, as I understand, sir.

MRS. BARTHWICK : It's to be hoped he will get a severe punishment.

SNOW : The odd thing is, sir, that he persists in sayin' he took the box himself.

BARTHWICK : Took the box himself! [*He smiles.*] What does he think to gain by that?

SNOW : He says the young gentleman was intoxicated last night—[JACK *stops the cracking of a nut, and looks at* SNOW. BARTHWICK, *losing his smile, has put his wine-glass down; there is a silence*— SNOW, *looking from face to face, remarks*]—took him into the house and gave him whisky; and under the influence of an empty stomach the man says he took the box.

MRS. BARTHWICK : The impudent wretch!

BARTHWICK : D' you mean that he—er—intends to put this forward to-morrow?

SNOW : That'll be his line, sir; but whether he's endeavouring to shield his wife, or whether [*he looks at* JACK] there's something in it, will be for the magistrate to say.

MRS. BARTHWICK : [*Haughtily.*] Something in what? I don't understand you. As if my son would bring a man like that into the house!

BARTHWICK : [*From the fireplace, with an effort to be calm.*] My son can speak for himself, no doubt. Well, Jack, what do you say?

MRS. BARTHWICK : [*Sharply.*] What does he say? Why, of course, he says the whole story's stuff!

JACK : [*Embarrassed.*] Well, of course, I—of course, I don't know anything about it.

MRS. BARTHWICK : I should think not, indeed! [*To* SNOW.] The man is an audacious ruffian!

BARTHWICK : [*Suppressing jumps.*] But in view of my son's saying there's nothing in this—this fable—will it be necessary to proceed against the man under the circumstances?

SNOW : We shall have to charge him with the assault, sir. It would be as well for your son to come down to the Court. There'll be a remand, no doubt.

The queer thing is there was quite a sum of money found on him, and a crimson silk purse. [BARTHWICK *starts;* JACK *rises and sits down again.*] I suppose the lady hasn't missed her purse?

BARTHWICK : [*Hastily.*] Oh, no! Oh! No!

JACK : No!

MRS. BARTHWICK : [*Dreamily.*] No! [*To* SNOW.] I've been inquiring of the servants. This man *does* hang about the house. I shall feel much safer if he gets a good long sentence; I do think we ought to be protected against such ruffians.

BARTHWICK : Yes, yes, of course, on principle—but in this case we have a number of things to think of. [*To* SNOW.] I suppose, as you say, the man must be charged, eh?

SNOW : No question about that, sir.

BARTHWICK : [*Staring gloomily at* JACK.] This prosecution goes very much against the grain with me. I have great sympathy with the poor. In my position I'm bound to recognise the distress there is amongst them. The condition of the people leaves much to be desired. D'you follow me? I wish I could see my way to drop it.

MRS. BARTHWICK : [*Sharply.*] John! it's simply not

fair to other people. It's putting property at the mercy of any one who likes to take it.

BARTHWICK : [*Trying to make signs to her aside.*] I'm not defending him, not at all. I'm trying to look at the matter broadly.

MRS. BARTHWICK : Nonsense, John, there's a time for everything.

SNOW : [*Rather sardonically.*] I might point out, sir, that to withdraw the charge of stealing would not make much difference, because the facts must come out [*he looks significantly at* JACK] in reference to the assault; and as I said that charge will have to go forward.

BARTHWICK : [*Hastily.*] Yes, oh! exactly! It's entirely on the woman's account—entirely a matter of my own private feelings.

SNOW : If I were you, sir, I should let things take their course. It's not likely there'll be much difficulty. These things are very quick settled.

BARTHWICK : [*Doubtfully.*] You think so—you think so?

JACK : [*Rousing himself.*] I say, what shall I have to swear to?

SNOW : That's best known to yourself, sir. [*Retreating to the door.*] Better employ a solicitor, sir, in case anything should arise. We shall have the butler to prove the loss of the article. You'll excuse me going, I'm rather pressed to-night. The case may come on any time after eleven. Good evening, sir; good evening, ma'am. I shall have to produce the box in court to-morrow, so if you'll excuse me, sir, I may as well take it with me.

[*He takes the silver box and leaves them with a little bow.*]

[BARTHWICK *makes a move to follow him, then dashing his hands beneath his coat tails, speaks with desperation.*]

BARTHWICK : I do wish you'd leave me to manage things myself. You *will* put your nose into matters you know nothing of. A pretty mess you've made of this!

MRS. BARTHWICK : [*Coldly.*] I don't in the least know what you're talking about. If you can't stand up for your rights, I can. I've no patience with your principles, it's such nonsense.

BARTHWICK : Principles! Good Heavens! What have principles to do with it for goodness sake? Don't you know that Jack was drunk last night!

JACK : Dad!

MRS. BARTHWICK : [*In horror rising.*] Jack!

JACK : Look here, Mother—I had supper. Everybody does. I mean to say—you know what I mean—it's absurd to call it being drunk. At Oxford everybody gets a bit "on" sometimes——

MRS. BARTHWICK : Well, I think it's most dreadful! If that is really what you do at Oxford——

JACK : [*Angrily.*] Well, why did you send me there? One must do as other fellows do. It's such nonsense, I mean, to call it being drunk. Of course I'm awfully sorry. I've had such a beastly headache all day.

BARTHWICK : Tcha! If you'd only had the common decency to remember what happened when you came in. Then we should know what truth there was in what this fellow says—as it is, it's all the most confounded darkness.

JACK : [*Staring as though at half-formed visions.*] I just get a— and then—it's gone——

MRS. BARTHWICK : Oh, Jack! do you mean to say you were so tipsy you can't even remember——

JACK : Look here, Mother! Of course I remember I came—I must have come——

BARTHWICK : [*Unguardedly, and walking up and down.*] Tcha!—and that infernal purse! Good Heavens! It'll get into the papers. Who on earth could have foreseen a thing like this? Better to have lost a dozen cigarette-boxes, and said nothing about it. [*To his wife.*] It's all your doing. I told you so from the first. I wish to goodness Roper would come!

MRS. BARTHWICK : [*Sharply.*] I don't know what you're talking about, John.

BARTHWICK : [*Turning on her.*] No, you—you—you don't know anything! [*Sharply.*] Where the devil is Roper? If he can see a way out of this he's a better man than I take him for. I defy *any one* to see a way out of it. *I* can't.

JACK : Look here, don't excite Dad—I can simply say I was too beastly tired, and don't remember anything except that I came in and [in a dying voice] went to bed the same as usual.

BARTHWICK : Went to bed? Who knows where you went—I've lost all confidence. For all I know you slept on the floor.

JACK : [*Indignantly.*] I didn't, I slept on the——

BARTHWICK : [Sitting on the sofa.] Who cares where you slept; what does it matter if he mentions the—the—a perfect disgrace?

MRS. BARTHWICK : What? [*A silence.*] I *insist* on knowing.

JACK : Oh! nothing——

MRS. BARTHWICK : Nothing? What do you mean by nothing, Jack? There's your father in such a state about it!——

JACK : It's only my purse.

MRS. BARTHWICK : Your purse! You know perfectly well you haven't got one.

JACK : Well, it was somebody else's—it was all a joke—I didn't want the beastly thing——

MRS. BARTHWICK : Do you mean that you had another person's purse, and that this man took it too?

BARTHWICK : Tcha! Of course he took it too! A man like that Jones will make the most of it. It'll get into the papers.

MRS. BARTHWICK : I don't understand. What on earth is all the fuss about? [*Bending over* JACK, *and softly*.] Jack now, tell me dear! Don't be afraid. What is it? Come!

JACK : Oh, don't Mother!

MRS. BARTHWICK : But don't what, dear?

JACK : It was pure sport. I don't know how I got the thing. Of course I'd had a bit of a row—I didn't know what I was doing—I was—I was—well, you know—I suppose I must have pulled the bag out of her hand.

MRS. BARTHWICK : Out of her hand? Whose hand? What bag—whose bag?

JACK : Oh! I don't know—*her* bag—it belonged to—[*in a desperate and rising voice*] a woman.

MRS. BARTHWICK : A woman? *Oh! Jack! No!*

JACK : [*Jumping up.*] You *would* have it. I didn't want to tell you. It's not my fault.

[*The door opens and* MARLOW *ushers in a man of middle age, inclined to corpulence, in evening dress. He has a ruddy, thin moustache, and dark, quick-moving little eyes. His eyebrows are Chinese.*]

MARLOW : Mr. Roper, sir. [*He leaves the room.*]

ROPER : [*With a quick look round.*] How do you do?

[*But neither* JACK *nor* MRS. BARTHWICK *make a sign.*]

BARTHWICK : [*Hurrying.*] Thank goodness you've come, Roper. You remember what I told you this afternoon; we've just had the detective here.

ROPER : Got the box?

BARTHWICK : Yes, yes, but look here—it wasn't the charwoman at all; her drunken loafer of a husband took the things—he says that fellow there—[*he waves his hand at* JACK, *who with his shoulder raised, seems trying to ward off a blow*]—

let him into the house last night. Can you imagine such a thing.

[ROPER *laughs.*]

BARTHWICK : [*With excited emphasis.*]. It's no laughing matter, Roper. I told you about that business of Jack's too—don't you see—the brute took both the things—took that infernal purse. It'll get into the papers.

ROPER : [*Raising his eyebrows.*] H'm! The purse! Depravity in high life! What does your son say?

BARTHWICK : He remembers nothing. D—n! Did you ever see such a mess? It'll get into the papers.

MRS. BARTHWICK : [*With her hand across her eyes.*] Oh! it's not that——

[BARTHWICK *and* ROPER *turn and look at her.*]

BARTHWICK : It's the idea of that woman—she's just heard——

[ROPER *nods. And* MRS. BARTHWICK, *setting her lips, gives a slow look at* JACK, *and sits down at the table.*]

What on earth's to be done, Roper? A ruffian like this Jones will make all the capital he can out of that purse.

MRS. BARTHWICK : I don't believe that Jack took that purse.

BARTHWICK : What—when the woman came here for it this morning?

MRS. BARTHWICK : Here? She had the impudence? Why wasn't I told?

[*She looks round from face to face—no one answers her, there is a pause.*]

BARTHWICK : [*Suddenly.*] What's to be done, Roper?

ROPER : [*Quietly to* JACK.] I suppose you didn't leave your latch-key in the door?

JACK : [*Sullenly.*] Yes, I did.

BARTHWICK : Good heavens! What next?

MRS. BARTHWICK : I'm certain you never let that man into the house, Jack, it's a wild invention. I'm sure there's not a word of truth in it, Mr. Roper.

ROPER : [*Very suddenly.*] Where did you sleep last night?

JACK : [*Promptly.*] On the sofa, there—[*hesitating*]—that is—I——

BARTHWICK : On the sofa? D' you mean to say you didn't go to bed?

JACK : [*Sullenly.*] No.

BARTHWICK : If you don't remember anything, how can you remember that?

JACK : Because I woke up there in the morning.

MRS. BARTHWICK : Oh, Jack!

BARTHWICK : Good Gracious!

JACK : And Mrs. Jones saw me. I wish you wouldn't bait me so.

ROPER : Do you remember giving any one a drink?

JACK : By Jove, I do seem to remember a fellow with—a fellow with [*He looks at* ROPER.] I say, d'you want me——?

ROPER : [*Quick as lightning.*] With a dirty face?

JACK : [*With illumination.*] I do—I distinctly remember his——

[BARTHWICK *moves abruptly;* MRS. BARTHWICK *looks at* ROPER *angrily, and touches her son's arm.*]

MRS. BARTHWICK : You don't remember, it's ridiculous! I don't believe the man was ever here at all.

BARTHWICK : You must speak the truth, if it is the truth. But if you do remember such a dirty business, I shall wash my hands of you altogether.

JACK : [*Glaring at them.*] Well, what the devil——

MRS. BARTHWICK : Jack!

JACK : Well, Mother, I—I don't know what you do want.

MRS. BARTHWICK : We want you to speak the truth and say you never let this low man into the house.

BARTHWICK : Of course if you think that you really gave this man whisky in that disgraceful way, and let him see what you'd been doing, and were in such a disgusting condition that you don't remember a word of it——

ROPER : [*Quick.*] I've no memory myself—never had.

BARTHWICK : [*Desperately.*] I don't know what you're to say.

ROPER : [*To* JACK.] Say nothing at all! Don't put yourself in a false position. The man stole the things or the woman stole the things, you had nothing to do with it. You were asleep on the sofa.

MRS. BARTHWICK : Your leaving the latch-key in the door was quite bad enough, there's no need to mention anything else. [*Touching his forehead softly.*] My dear, how hot your head is!

JACK : But I want to know what I'm to do. [*Passionately.*] I won't be badgered like this.

[MRS. BARTHWICK *recoils from him.*]

ROPER : [*Very quickly.*] You forget all about it. You were asleep.

JACK : Must I go down to the Court to-morrow?

ROPER : [*Shaking his head.*] No.

BARTHWICK : [*In a relieved voice.*] Is that so?

ROPER : Yes.

BARTHWICK : But you'll go, Roper.

ROPER : Yes.

JACK : [*With wan cheerfulness.*] Thanks, awfully! So long as I don't have to go. [*Putting his hand up to his head.*] I think if you'll excuse me—I've had a most beastly day. [*He looks from his father to his mother.*]

MRS. BARTHWICK : [*Turning quickly.*] Goodnight, my boy.

JACK : Good-night, Mother.

[*He goes out.* MRS. BARTHWICK *heaves a sigh. There is a silence.*]

BARTHWICK : He gets off too easily. But for my money that woman would have prosecuted him.

ROPER : You find money useful.

BARTHWICK : I've my doubts whether we ought to hide the truth——

ROPER : There'll be a remand.

BARTHWICK : What! D'you mean he'll have to appear on the remand.

ROPER : Yes.

BARTHWICK : H'm, I thought you'd be able to—— Look here, Roper, you must keep that purse out of the papers.

[ROPER *fixes his little eyes on him and nods.*]

MRS. BARTHWICK : Mr. Roper, don't you think the magistrate ought to be told what sort of people these Jones's are; I mean about their immorality before they were married. I don't know if John told you.

ROPER : Afraid it's not material.

MRS. BARTHWICK : Not material?

ROPER : Purely private life! May have happened to the magistrate.

BARTHWICK : [*With a movement as if to shift a burden.*] Then you'll take the thing into your hands?

ROPER : If the gods are kind. [*He holds his hand out.*]

BARTHWICK : [*Shaking it dubiously.*] Kind eh? What? You going?

ROPER : Yes. I've another case, something like yours—most unexpected.

[*He bows to* MRS. BARTHWICK, *and goes out, followed by* BARTHWICK, *talking to the last.* MRS. BARTHWICK *at the table bursts into smothered sobs.* BARTHWICK *returns.*]

BARTHWICK : [*To himself.*] There'll be a scandal!

MRS. BARTHWICK : [*Disguising her grief at once.*] I simply can't imagine what Roper means by making a joke of a thing like that!

BARTHWICK : [*Staring strangely.*] You! You can't imagine anything! You've no more imagination than a fly!

MRS. BARTHWICK : [*Angrily.*] You dare to tell me that I have no imagination.

BARTHWICK : [*Flustered.*] I—I'm upset. From beginning to end, the whole thing has been utterly against my principles.

MRS. BARTHWICK : Rubbish! You haven't any! Your principles are nothing in the world but sheer fright!

BARTHWICK : [*Walking to the window.*] I've never been frightened in my life. You heard what Roper said. It's enough to upset one when a thing like this happens. Everything one says and does seems to turn in one's mouth—it's—it's uncanny. It's not the sort of thing I've been accustomed to. [*As though stifling, he throws the window open. The faint sobbing of a child comes in.*] What's that?

[*They listen.*]

MRS. BARTHWICK : [*Sharply.*] I can't stand that crying. I must send Marlow to stop it. My nerves are all on edge. [*She rings the bell.*]

BARTHWICK : I'll shut the window; you'll hear nothing. [*He shuts the window. There is silence.*]

MRS. BARTHWICK : [*Sharply.*] That's no good! It's on my nerves. Nothing upsets me like a child's crying.

[MARLOW *comes in.*]

What's that noise of crying, Marlow? It sounds like a child.

BARTHWICK : It is a child. I can see it against the railings.

MARLOW : [*Opening the window, and looking out quietly.*] It's Mrs. Jones's little boy, ma'am; he came here after his mother.

MRS. BARTHWICK : [*Moving quickly to the window.*] Poor little chap! John, we oughtn't to go on with this!

BARTHWICK : [*Sitting heavily in a chair.*] Ah! but it's out of our hands!

[MRS. BARTHWICK *turns her back to the window. There is an expression of distress on her face. She stands motionless, compressing her lips. The crying begins again.* BARTHWICK *covers his ears with his hands, and* MARLOW *shuts the window. The crying ceases.*]

The curtain falls.

ACT III

Eight days have passed, and the scene is a London Police Court at one o'clock. A canopied seat of Justice is surmounted by the lion and unicorn. Before the fire a worn-looking MAGISTRATE *is warming his coat-tails, and staring at two little girls in faded blue and orange rags, who are placed before the dock. Close to the witness-box is a* RELIEVING OFFICER *in an overcoat, and a short brown beard. Beside the little girls stands a bald* POLICE CONSTABLE. *On the front bench are sitting* BARTHWICK *and* ROPER, *and behind them* JACK. *In the railed enclosure are seedy-looking men and women. Some prosperous constables sit or stand about.*

MAGISTRATE : [*In his paternal and ferocious voice, hissing hiss's.*] Now let us dispose of these young ladies.

USHER : Theresa Livens, Maud Livens.

[*The bald* CONSTABLE *indicates the little girls, who remain silent, disillusioned, inattentive.*]

Relieving Officer!

[*The* RELIEVING OFFICER *steps into the witness-box.*]

USHER : The evidence you give to the Court shall be the truth, the whole truth, and nothing but the truth, so help you God! Kiss the book!

[*The book is kissed.*]

RELIEVING OFFICER : [*In a monotone, pausing slightly at each sentence end, that his evidence may be inscribed.*] About ten o'clock this morning, your Worship, I found these two little girls in Blue Street, Fulham, crying outside a public-house. Asked where their home was, they said they had no home. Mother had gone away. Asked about their father. Their father had no work. Asked where they slept last night. At their aunt's. I've made inquiries, your Worship. The wife has broken up the home and gone on the streets. The husband is out of work and living in common lodging-houses. The husband's sister has eight children of her own, and says she can't afford to keep these little girls any longer.

MAGISTRATE : [*Returning to his seat beneath the canopy of justice.*] Now, let me see. You say the mother is on the streets; what evidence have you of that?

RELIEVING OFFICER : I have the husband here, your Worship.

MAGISTRATE : Very well; then let us see him.

[*There are cries of* "LIVENS." *The* MAGISTRATE *leans forward, and stares with hard compassion at the little girls.* LIVENS *comes in. He is quiet, with grizzled hair, and a muffler for a collar. He stands beside the witness-box.*]

And you, are their father? Now, why don't you keep your little girls at home. How is it you leave them to wander about the streets like this?

LIVENS : I've got no home, your Worship. I'm living from 'and to mouth. I've got no work; and nothin' to keep them on.

MAGISTRATE : How is that?

LIVENS : [*Ashamedly.*] My wife, she broke my 'ome up, and pawned the things.

MAGISTRATE : But what made you let her?

LEVINS : Your Worship, I'd no chance to stop 'er, she did it when I was out lookin' for work.

MAGISTRATE : Did you ill-treat her?

LIVENS : [*Emphatically.*] I never raised my 'and to her in my life, your Worship.

MAGISTRATE : Then what was it—did she drink?

LIVENS : Yes, your Worship.

MAGISTRATE : Was she loose in her behaviour?

LIVENS : [*In a low voice.*] Yes, your Worship.

MAGISTRATE : And where is she now?

LIVENS : I don't know your Worship. She went off with a man, and after that I——

MAGISTRATE : Yes, yes. Who knows anything of her? [*To the bald* CONSTABLE.] Is she known here?

RELIEVING OFFICER : Not in this district, your Worship; but I have ascertained that she is well known——

MAGISTRATE : Yes—yes; we'll stop at that. Now [*To the Father*] you say that she has broken up your home, and left these little girls. What provision can you make for them? You look a strong man.

LIVENS : So I am, your Worship. I'm willin' enough to work, but for the life of me I can't get anything to do.

MAGISTRATE : But have you tried?

LIVENS : I've tried everything, your Worship—I've tried my 'ardest.

MAGISTRATE : Well, well—— [*There is a silence.*]

RELIEVING OFFICER : If your Worship thinks it's a case, my people are willing to take them.

MAGISTRATE : Yes, yes, I know; but I've no evidence that this man is not the proper guardian for his children.

[*He rises and goes back to the fire.*]

RELIEVING OFFICER : The mother, your Worship, is able to get access to them.

MAGISTRATE : Yes, yes; the mother, of course, is an improper person to have anything to do with them. [*To the Father.*] Well, now what do you say?

LIVENS : Your Worship, I can only say that if I could get work I should be only too willing to provide for them. But what can I do, your Worship? Here I am obliged to live from 'and to mouth in these 'ere common lodging-houses. I'm a strong man—I'm willing to work —I'm half as alive again as some of 'em—but you see, your Worship, my 'airs' turned a bit, owing to the fever—[*Touches his hair*]—and that's against me; and I don't seem to get a chance anyhow.

MAGISTRATE : Yes—yes. [*Slowly.*] Well, I think it's a case. [*Staring his hardest at the little girls.*] Now, are you willing that these little girls should be sent to a home.

LIVENS : Yes, your Worship, I should be very willing.

MAGISTRATE : Well, I'll remand them for a week. Bring them again to-day week; if I see no reason against it then, I'll make an order.

RELIEVING OFFICER : To-day week, your Worship.

[*The bald* CONSTABLE *takes the little girls out by the shoulders. The father follows them. The* MAGISTRATE, *returning to his seat, bends over and talks to his* CLERK *inaudibly.*]

BARTHWICK : [*Speaking behind his hand.*] A painful case, Roper; very distressing state of things.

ROPER : Hundreds like this in the Police Courts.

BARTHWICK : Most distressing! The more I see of it, the more important this question of the condition of the people seems to become. I shall certainly make a point of taking up the cudgels in the House. I shall move——

[*The* MAGISTRATE *ceases talking to his* CLERK.]

CLERK : Remands!

[BARTHWICK *stops abruptly. There is a stir and* MRS. JONES *comes in by the public door;* JONES, *ushered by policemen, comes from the prisoner's door. They file into the dock.*]

CLERK : James Jones, Jane Jones.

USHER : Jane Jones!

BARTHWICK : [*In a whisper.*] The purse—the purse must be kept out of it, Roper. Whatever happens you must keep that out of the papers.

[ROPER *nods.*]

BALD CONSTABLE : Hush!

[MRS. JONES, *dressed in a thin, black, wispy dress, and black straw hat, stands motionless with hands crossed on the front rail of the dock.* JONES *leans against the back rail of the dock, and keeps half turning, glancing defiantly about him. He is haggard and unshaven.*]

CLERK : [*Consulting with his papers.*] This is the case remanded from last Wednesday, sir. Theft of a silver cigarette-box and assault on the police; the two charges were taken together. Jane Jones! James Jones!

MAGISTRATE : [*Staring.*] Yes, yes; I remember.

CLERK : Jane Jones.

MRS. JONES : Yes, sir.

CLERK : Do you admit stealing a silver cigarette-box valued at five pounds, ten shillings, from the house of John BARTHWICK, M.P., between the hours of 11 p.m. on Easter Monday and 8.45 a.m. on Easter Tuesday last? Yes, or no?

MRS. JONES : [*In a logy voice.*] No, sir, I do not, sir.

CLERK : James Jones? Do you admit stealing a silver

cigarette-box valued at five pounds, ten shillings, from the house of John BARTHWICK, M.P., between the hours of 11 p.m. on Easter Monday and 8.45 a.m. on Easter Tuesday last. And further making an assault on the police when in the execution of their duty at 3 p.m. on Easter Tuesday? Yes or no?

JONES : [*Sullenly.*] Yes, but I've got a lot to say about it.

MAGISTRATE : [*To the* CLERK.] Yes—yes. But how comes it that these two people are charged with the same offence? Are they husband and wife?

CLERK : Yes, sir. You remember you ordered a remand for further evidence as to the story of the male prisoner.

MAGISTRATE : Have they been in custody since?

CLERK : You released the woman on her own recognisances, sir.

MAGISTRATE : Yes, yes, this is the case of the silver box; I remember now. Well?

CLERK : Thomas Marlow.

[*The cry of* "THOMAS MARLOW" *is repeated* MARLOW *comes in, and steps into the witness-box.*]

USHER : The evidence you give to the court shall be the truth, the whole truth, and nothing but the truth, so help you God. Kiss the book.

[*The book is kissed. The silver box is handed up, and placed on the rail.*]

CLERK : [*Reading from his papers.*] Your name is Thomas Marlow? Are you, butler to John BARTHWICK, M.P., of 6, Rockingham Gate?

MARLOW : Yes, sir.

CLERK : Is that the box?

MARLOW : Yes sir.

CLERK : And did you miss the same at 8.45 on the following morning, on going to remove the tray?

MARLOW : Yes, sir.

CLERK : Is the female prisoner known to you?

[MARLOW *nods.*]

Is she the charwoman employed at 6, Rockingham Gate?

[*Again* MARLOW *nods.*]

Did you at the time of your missing the box find her in the room alone?

MARLOW : Yes, sir.

CLERK : Did you afterwards communicate the loss to your employer, and did he send you to the police station?

MARLOW : Yes, sir.

CLERK : [*To* MRS. JONES.] Have you anything to ask him?

MRS. JONES : No, sir, nothing, thank you, sir.

CLERK : [*To* JONES.] James Jones, have you anything to ask this witness?

JONES : I don't know 'im.

MAGISTRATE : Are you sure you put the box in the place you say at the time you say?

MARLOW : Yes, your Worship.

MAGISTRATE : Very well; then now let us have the officer.

[MARLOW *leaves the box, and* SNOW *goes into it.*]

USHER : The evidence you give to the court shall be the truth, the whole truth, and nothing but the truth, so help you God. [*The book is kissed.*]

CLERK : [*Reading from his papers.*] Your name is Robert Allow? You are a detective in the X. B. division of the Metropolitan police force? According to instructions received did you on Easter Tuesday last proceed to the prisoner's lodgings at 34, Merthyr Street, St. Soames's? And did you on entering see the box produced, lying on the table?

SNOW : Yes, sir.

CLERK : Is that the box?

SNOW : [*Fingering the box.*] Yes, sir.

CLERK : And did you thereupon take possession of it, and charge the female prisoner with theft of the box from 6, Rockingham Gate? And did she deny the same?

SNOW : Yes, sir.

CLERK : Did you take her into custody?

SNOW : Yes, sir.

MAGISTRATE : What was her behaviour?

SNOW : Perfectly quiet, your Worship. She persisted in the denial. That's all.

MAGISTRATE : *Do* you know her?

SNOW : No, your Worship.

MAGISTRATE : Is she known here?

BALD CONSTABLE : No, your Worship, they're neither of them known, we've nothing against them at all.

CLERK : [*To* MRS. JONES.] Have you anything to ask the officer?

MRS. JONES : No, sir, thank you, I've nothing to ask him.

MAGISTRATE : Very well then—go on.

CLERK : [*Reading from his papers.*] And while you were taking the female prisoner did the male prisoner interpose, and endeavour to hinder you in the execution of your duty, and did he strike you a blow?

SNOW : Yes, sir.

CLERK : And did he say, "You, let her go, I took the box myself"?

SNOW : He did.

CLERK : And did you blow your whistle and obtain the assistance of another constable, and take him into custody?

SNOW : I did.

CLERK : Was he violent on the way to the station, and did he use bad language, and did he several times repeat that he had taken the box himself? [SNOW *nods.*] Did you thereupon ask him in what manner he had stolen the box? And did you understand him to say he had entered the house at the invitation of young Mr. BARTHWICK— [BARTHWICK, *turning in his seat, frowns at ROPER.*]—after midnight on Easter Monday, and partaken of whisky, and that under the influence of the whisky he had taken the box?

SNOW : I did, sir.

CLERK : And was his demeanour throughout very violent?

SNOW : It was very violent.

JONES : [*Breaking in.*] Violent—-of course it was! You put your 'ands on my wife when I kept tellin' you I took the thing myself.

MAGISTRATE : [*Hissing, with protruded neck.*] Now—you will have your chance of saying what you want to say presently. Have you anything to ask the officer?

JONES : [*Sullenly.*] No.

MAGISTRATE : Very well then. Now let us hear what the female prisoner has to say first.

MRS. JONES : Well, your Worship, of course I can only say what I've said all along, that I didn't take the box.

MAGISTRATE : Yes, but did you know that it was taken?

MRS. JONES : No, your Worship. And, of course, to what my husband says, your Worship, I can't speak of my own knowledge. Of course, I know that he came home very late on the Monday night. It was past one o'clock when he came in, and he was not himself at all.

MAGISTRATE : Had he been drinking?

MRS. JONES : Yes, your Worship.

MAGISTRATE : And was he drunk?

MRS. JONES : Yes, your Worship, he was almost quite drunk.

MAGISTRATE : And did he say anything to you?

MRS. JONES : No, your Worship, only to call me names. And of course in the morning when I got up and went to work he was asleep. And I don't know anything more about it until I came home again. Except that Mr. BARTHWICK—that's my employer, your Worship—told me the box was missing.

MAGISTRATE : Yes, yes.

MRS. JONES : But of course when I was shaking out my husband's coat the cigarette-box fell out and all the cigarettes were scattered on the bed.

MAGISTRATE : You say all the cigarettes were scattered on the bed? [*To* SNOW.] Did you see the cigarettes scattered on the bed?

SNOW : No, your Worship, I did not.

MAGISTRATE : You see he says he didn't see them.

JONES ; Well, they were there for all that.

SNOW : I can't say, your Worship, that I had the

opportunity of going round the room; I had all my work cut out with the male prisoner.

MAGISTRATE : [*To* MRS. JONES.] Well, what more have you to say?

MRS. JONES : Of course when I saw the box, your Worship, I was dreadfully upset, and I couldn't think why he had done such a thing; when the officer came we were having words about it, because it is ruin to me, your Worship, in my profession, and I have three little children dependent on me.

MAGISTRATE : [*Protruding his neck*]. Yes—yes—but what did he say to you?

MRS. JONES : I asked him whatever came over him to do such a thing—and he said it was the drink. He said he had had too much to drink, and something came over him. And of course, your Worship, he had had very little to eat all day, and the drink does go to the head when you have not had enough to eat. Your Worship may not know, but it is the truth. And I would like to say that all through his married life, I have never known him to do such a thing before, though we have passed through great hardships and [*speaking with soft emphasis*] I am quite sure he would not have done it if he had been himself at the time.

MAGISTRATE : Yes, yes. But don't you know that that is no excuse?

MRS. JONES : Yes, your Worship. I know that it is no excuse.

[*The* MAGISTRATE *leans over and parleys with his* CLERK.]

JACK : [*Leaning over from his seat behind.*] I say, Dad——

BARTHWICK : Tsst! [*Sheltering his mouth he speaks to* ROPER.] Roper, you had better get up now and say that considering the circumstances and the poverty of the prisoners, we have no wish to proceed any further, and if the magistrate would deal with the case as one of disorder only on the part of——

BALD CONSTABLE : HSSShh!

[ROPER *shakes his head.*]

MAGISTRATE : Now, supposing what you say and what your husband says is true, what I have to consider is—how did he obtain access to this house, and were you in any way a party to his obtaining access? You are the charwoman employed at the house?

MRS. JONES : Yes, your Worship, and of course if I had let him into the house it would have been very wrong of me; and I have never done such a thing in any of the houses where I have been employed.

MAGISTRATE : Well—so you say. Now let us hear what story the male prisoner makes of it.

JONES : [*Who leans with his arms on the dock behind, speaks in a slow, sullen voice.*] Wot I say is wot my wife says. I've never been 'ad up in a police court before, an' I can prove I took it when in liquor. I told her, and she can tell you the same, that I was goin' to throw the thing into the water sooner then 'ave it on my mind.

MAGISTRATE : But how did you get into the *house*?

JONES : I was passin'. I was goin' 'ome from the "Goat and Bells."

MAGISTRATE : The "Goat and Bells,"—what is that? A public-house?

JONES . Yes, at the corner. It was Bank 'oliday, an' I'd 'ad a drop to drink. I see this young Mr. BARTHWICK tryin' to find the keyhole on the wrong side of the door.

MAGISTRATE : Well?

JONES : [*Slowly and with many pauses.*] Well—I 'elped 'im to find it—drunk as a lord 'e was. He goes on, an' comes back again, and says, I've got nothin' for you, 'e says, but come in an' 'ave a drink. So I went in just as you might 'ave done yourself. We 'ad a drink o' whisky just as you might have 'ad, 'nd young Mr. BARTHWICK says to me, "Take a drink 'nd a smoke. Take anything you like, 'e says." And then he went to sleep on the sofa. I 'ad some more whisky—an' I 'ad a smoke—and I 'ad some more whisky—an' I carn't tell yer what 'appened after that.

MAGISTRATE : Do you mean to say that you were so drunk that you can remember nothing?

JACK : [*Softly to his father.*] I say, that's exactly what——

BARTHWICK : TSSh!

JONES : That's what I do mean.

MAGISTRATE : And yet you say you stole the box?

JONES : I never stole the box. I took it.

MAGISTRATE : [*Hissing with protruded neck.*] You did not steal it— you took it. Did it belong to you—what is that but stealing?

JONES : I took it.

MAGISTRATE : You took it—you took it away from their house and you took it to your house——

JONES : [*Sullenly breaking in.*] I ain't got a house.

MAGISTRATE : Very well, let us hear what this young man Mr.—Mr. BARTHWICK has to say to your story.

[SNOW *leaves the witness-box. The* BALD CONSTABLE *beckons* JACK, *who, clutching his hat, goes into the witness-box.* ROPER *moves to the table set apart for his profession.*]

SWEARING CLERK : The evidence you give to the court shall be the truth, the whole truth, and nothing but the truth, so help you God. Kiss the book.

[*The book is kissed.*]

ROPER : [*Examining.*] What is your name?

JACK : [*In a low voice.*] John BARTHWICK, Junior.

[*The* CLERK *writes it down.*]

ROPER : Where do you live?

JACK : At 6, Rockingham Gate.

[*All his answers are recorded by the* CLERK.]

ROPER : You are the son of the owner?

JACK : [*In a very low voice.*] Yes.

ROPER : Speak up, please. Do you know the prisoners?

JACK : [*Looking at the* JONESES, *in a low voice.*] I've seen Mrs. Jones. I [*in a loud voice*] don't know the man.

JONES : Well, I know you!

BALD CONSTABLE : HSSh!

ROPER : Now, did you come in late on the night of Easter Monday?

JACK : Yes.

ROPER : And did you by mistake leave your latch key in the door?

JACK : Yes.

MAGISTRATE : Oh! You left your latch-key in the door?

ROPER : And is that all you can remember about your coming in?

JACK : [*In a loud voice.*] Yes, it is.

MAGISTRATE : Now, you have heard the male prisoner's story, what do you say to that?

JACK : [*Turning to the* MAGISTRATE, *speaks suddenly in a confident, straight-forward voice.*] The fact of the matter is, sir, that I'd been out to the theatre that night, and had supper afterwards, and I came in late.

MAGISTRATE : Do you remember this man being outside when you came in?

JACK. No, sir : [*He hesitates.*] I don't think I do.

MAGISTRATE : [*Somewhat puzzled.*] Well, did he help

you to open the door, as he says? Did any one help you to open the door?

JACK : No, sir—I don't think so, sir—I don't know.

MAGISTRATE : You don't know? But you must know. It isn't a usual thing for you to have the door opened for you, is it?

JACK : [*With a shamefaced smile.*] No.

MAGISTRATE : Very well, then——

JACK : [*Desperately.*] The fact of the matter is, sir, I'm afraid I'd had too much champagne that night.

MAGISTRATE : [*Smiling.*] Oh! you'd had too much champagne?

JONES : May I ask the gentleman a question?

MAGISTRATE : Yes—yes—you may ask him what questions you like.

JONES : Don't you remember you said you was a Liberal, same as your father, and you asked me wot I was?

JACK : [*With his hand against his brow.*] I seem to remember——

JONES : And I said to you, "I'm a bloomin' Conservative," I said; an' you said to me, "You look more like one of these 'ere Socialists. Take wotever you like," you said.

JACK : [*With sudden resolution.*] No, I don't. I don't remember anything of the sort.

JONES : Well, I do, an' my word's as good as yours. I've never been had up in a police court before. Look 'ere, don't you remember you had a sky-blue bag in your 'and [BARTHWICK *jumps.*]

ROPER : I submit to your worship that these questions are hardly to the point, the prisoner having admitted that he himself does not remember anything. [*There is a smile on the face of Justice.*] It is a case of the blind leading the blind.

JONES : [*Violently.*] I've done no more than wot he 'as. I'm a poor man; I've got no money an' no friends—he's a toff—he can do wot I can't.

MAGISTRATE : Now, now? All this won't help you—you must be quiet. You say you took this box? Now, what made you take it? Were you pressed for money?

JONES : I'm always pressed for money.

MAGISTRATE : Was that the reason you took it?

JONES : No.

MAGISTRATE : [*To* SNOW.] Was anything found on him?

SNOW : Yes, your worship. There was six pounds twelve shillin's found on him, and this purse.

[*The red silk purse is handed to the* MAGISTRATE. BARTHWICK *rises from his seat, but hastily sits down again.*]

MAGISTRATE : [*Staring at the purse.*] Yes, yes—let me see [*There is a silence.*] No, no, I've nothing before me as to the purse. How did you come by all that money?

JONES : [*After a long pause, suddenly.*] I declines to say.

MAGISTRATE : But if you had all that money, what made you take this box?

JONES : I took it out of spite.

MAGISTRATE : [*Hissing, with protruded neck.*] You took it out of spite? Well now, that's something! But do you imagine you can go about the town taking things out of spite?

JONES : If you had my life, if you'd been out of work——

MAGISTRATE : Yes, yes; I know—because you're out of work you think it's an excuse for everything.

JONES : [*Pointing at* JACK.] You ask 'im wot made 'im take the——

ROPER : [*Quietly.*] Does your Worship require this witness in the box any longer?

MAGISTRATE : [*Ironically.*] I think not; he is hardly profitable.

[JACK *leaves the witness-box, and hanging his head, resumes his seat.*]

JONES : You ask 'im wot made 'im take the lady's——

[*But the* BALD CONSTABLE *catches him by the sleeve.*]

BALD CONSTABLE : SSSh!

MAGISTRATE : [*Emphatically.*] Now listen to me.

I've nothing to do with what he may or may not have taken. Why did you resist the police in the execution of their duty?

JONES : It warn't their duty to take my wife, a respectable woman, that 'adn't done nothing.

MAGISTRATE : But I say it was. What made you strike the officer a blow?

JONES : Any man would a struck 'im a blow. I'd strike 'im again, I would.

MAGISTRATE : You are not making your case any better by violence. How do you suppose we could get on if everybody behaved like you?

JONES : [*Leaning forward, earnestly.*] Well, wot, about 'er; who's to make up to 'er for this? Who's to give 'er back 'er good name?

MRS. JONES : Your Worship, it's the children that's

preying on his mind, because of course I've lost my work. And I've had to find another room owing to the scandal.

MAGISTRATE : Yes, yes, I know—but if he hadn't acted like this nobody would have suffered.

JONES : [*Glaring round at* JACK.] I've done no worse than wot 'e 'as. Wot I want to know is wot's goin' to be done to 'im.

[*The* BALD CONSTABLE *again says "HSSh"*]

ROPER : Mr. BARTHWICK wishes it known, your Worship, that considering the poverty of the prisoners, he does not press the charge as to the box. Perhaps your Worship would deal with the case as one of disorder.

JONES : I don't want it smothered up, I want it all dealt with fair —I want my rights——

MAGISTRATE : [*Rapping his desk.*] Now you have said all you have to say, and you will be quiet.

[*There is a silence; the* MAGISTRATE *bends over and parleys with his* CLERK.]

Yes, I think I may discharge the woman. [*In a kindly voice he addresses* MRS. JONES, *who stands unmoving with her hands crossed on the rail.*] It is very unfortunate for you that this man has behaved as he has. It is not the consequences to him but the consequences to you. You have been brought here twice, you have lost your work—[*He glares at* JONES]—and this is what always happens. Now you may go away, and I am very sorry it was necessary to bring you here at all.

MRS. JONES : [*Softly.*] Thank you very much, your Worship.

[*She leaves the dock, and looking back at* JONES, *twists her fingers and is still.*]

MAGISTRATE : Yes, yes, but I can't pass it over. Go away, there's a good woman.

[MRS. JONES *stands back. The* MAGISTRATE *leans his head on his hand; then raising it he speaks to* JONES.]

Now, listen to me. Do you wish the case to be settled here, or do you wish it to go before a jury?

JONES : [*Muttering.*] I don't want no jury.

MAGISTRATE : Very well then, I will deal with it here. [*After a pause.*] You have pleaded guilty to stealing this box——

JONES : Not to stealin'——

BALD CONSTABLE : HSSShh!

MAGISTRATE : And to assaulting the police——

JONES : Any man as was a man——

MAGISTRATE : Your conduct here has been most improper. You give the excuse that you were drunk when you stole the box. I tell you that is no excuse. If you choose to get drunk and break the law afterwards you must take the consequences. And let me tell you that men like you, who get drunk and give way to your spite or whatever it is that's in you, are—are—a nuisance to the community.

JACK : [*Leaning from his seat.*] Dad! that's what you said to me!

BARTHWICK : TSSt!

[*There is a silence, while the* MAGISTRATE *consults his* CLERK; JONES *leans forward waiting.*]

MAGISTRATE : This is your first offence, and I am going to give you a light sentence. [*Speaking sharply, but without expression.*] One month with hard labour.

[*He bends, and parleys with his* CLERK. *The* BALD CONSTABLE *and another help* JONES *from the dock.*]

JONES : [*Stopping and twisting round.*] Call this justice? What about 'im? 'E got drunk! 'E took the purse—'e took the purse but [*in a muffled shout*] it's 'is money got 'im off—*justice!*

[*The prisoner's door is shut on* JONES, *and from*

seedy-looking men and women comes a hoarse and whispering groan.]

MAGISTRATE : We will now adjourn for lunch! [*He rises from his seat.*]

[*The Court is in a stir.* ROPER *gets up and speaks to the reporter.* JACK, *throwing up his head, walks with a swagger to the corridor;* BARTHWICK *follows.*]

MRS. JONES : [*Turning to him with a humble gesture.*] Oh! sir!

[BARTHWICK *hesitates, then yielding to his nerves, he makes a shame-faced gesture of refusal, and hurries out of court.* MRS. JONES *stands looking after him.*]

The curtain falls.